Book 1

All-Star Cheerleaders

Tick Tock, Taylor!

Do your best and forget the rest!

For Kira

Kane Miller, A Division of EDC Publishing

Text copyright © Anastasia Suen, 2011
Illustrations copyright © Kane Miller, 2011

For information contact:
Kane Miller, A Division of EDC Publishing
PO Box 470663
Tulsa, OK 74147-0663
www.kanemiller.com
www.edcpub.com
www.usbornebooksandmore.com

Illustrations by Hazel Mitchell
Cover design by Kat Godard

Library of Congress Control Number: 2011922731

Printed in the United States of America
2 3 4 5 6 7 8 9 10
ISBN: 978-1-61067-000-5

First Competition

"I thought this day would never come," said Taylor to her best friend Abby. The two girls looked around the hallway of the sports arena. There were cheerleaders everywhere. They had come from across the state to compete. It was October – time for the first All-Star competition of the season.

"We're the oldest on the squad now," said Taylor.

"You and me and Sophia," said Abby.

"How could I forget about Sophia?" asked Taylor. She frowned as she looked at the cheerleader with the dark hair. Sophia was eight, too. She was also *very* bossy.

Taylor and Abby were wearing red, white, and blue cheerleader outfits. The long-sleeved top had the Big D Elite name sewn on the front. The short skirt had a V notch on one side so they could move easily. Everyone from the Big D Elite Gym had the same uniform. Taylor's wavy blonde hair was tied up into a ponytail. So was Abby's long red hair. They wore matching red, white, and blue bows in their hair.

"Are you ready for your makeup, Taylor?" asked Coach Tammy.

"Coming," said Taylor. She walked over and sat on the floor in front of her coach. Taylor closed her eyes. Coach Tammy put the gold and silver glitter eye shadow on her.

"Now for the lipstick," said Coach Tammy. Taylor opened her eyes. Then she puckered her lips. Coach Tammy painted them bright red.

"And your star," said Coach Tammy. She put a silver glitter star on Taylor's left cheek. "You're done!"

"Thanks, Coach Tammy," said Taylor.

"You're welcome," said Coach Tammy. She gave Taylor a big hug.

Taylor walked over to sit with the team.

"It's your turn, Abby," said Coach Tammy.

"Now you can look gorgeous, too," said Taylor.

"I'm already gorgeous," said Abby. She patted her hair like a movie star.

Taylor giggled.

Abby walked over and sat down in front of Coach Tammy. Taylor looked at the tinies sitting next to her. The tinies were the smallest. They were only in preschool. They were the youngest cheerleaders at the gym. The seniors were the oldest. They were already in high school.

Coach Tammy was in charge of the tinies and the minis at the Big D Elite Gym. The tinies didn't really compete. They were a show team. After the tinies cheered, each of them got a trophy to take home.

Taylor was a mini now, so it was all about points. Each time the team competed, they would be given points. There were points for stunts and tumbling and jumps. The team with the most points won the first place trophy. The other teams only won a plaque.

After Abby's makeup was done, she came over and sat with Taylor.

"Now you listen to me," said Sophia sternly.

Taylor turned and looked at Sophia. She

was wagging her finger at Brianna. Poor Brianna looked down at the floor.

"There she goes again," said Taylor, "making Brianna cry."

"I have to keep Emma away from her," said Abby. She waved at her red-haired sister. "Come and sit with me, Emma."

Emma stood up and came over. She was six, just like Brianna.

Taylor looked around. Coach Tammy was busy putting makeup on the tinies. "I'll get Brianna," said Taylor. She stood up and walked over to Brianna. "Come sit with us."

Brianna looked up at Taylor. Tears ran down her cheeks. "Okay," she sniffed, as she stood up.

"Be nice to the flyers, Sophia," said Taylor.

"Why?" asked Sophia.

"Yelling doesn't help," said Taylor.

"You think you're so good," said Sophia, "but you're not. Your back walkover is way too slow."

Taylor put her hands on her hips. "Coach Tammy isn't worried."

Sophia lifted her hand and flipped her ponytail. "Coach Tammy never worries."

Abby came over and stood next to Taylor. "Do your best and forget the rest," said Abby. "That's what Coach Tammy always says."

"That's not how you win," said Sophia. She walked up to Taylor and pointed her finger. "You're holding back the team."

"No, I'm not," said Taylor.

"Yes, you are," said Sophia. "If we lose, it's all your fault."

Line Up

"What!" said Taylor. She couldn't believe her ears.

"How can you say that?" asked Abby.

Clap, clap, clap!

Taylor turned around. Coach Tammy was standing behind her.

"Girls," said Coach Tammy. She clapped her hands one more time. Now all the girls were looking at her.

"It's time to go in and warm up," said

Coach Tammy.

"Yay!" said Taylor. She turned and looked at her squad. Sophia still had her arms crossed. *Why was she so mean?*

"Line up with your squad," said Coach Tammy.

The girls from Big D Elite stood up and started getting in line. The tinies' squad was named Glow. Taylor's mini squad was named Glitter.

There were two girls from the Big D Elite youth squad there, too. Sarah and Jess were on the Shine squad, but they also helped Coach Tammy with the tinies. Sarah and Jess helped the five tinies hold hands.

We have to hold hands, too, thought Taylor. She reached out and took Brianna's hand. This was Brianna's first year as a mini. Last year she had been a tiny.

Taylor looked at Abby. She was holding her sister Emma's hand.

"You know what to do, Glitter squad," said Coach Tammy.

"Yes, we do," said Taylor. She walked with Brianna and stood next to Coach Tammy. They would be the front of the line. Abby and Emma followed Taylor.

Now half of the Glitter squad was lined up. Taylor turned to see what the rest of them were doing.

Sophia was wagging her finger at Kayla. *What now?* thought Taylor.

"Kayla," said Taylor. "We're ready to go."

Kayla turned and looked at Taylor. She looked like she was going to cry. *Why is Sophia so bossy?* thought Taylor.

"Take Liv's hand," said Taylor.

Liv stood up and held her hand out. Kayla came over and held Liv's hand, then Liv and Kayla walked over and joined the line. Maddie lined up behind them. Then she held out her hand and Sophia took it. Sophia was at the end of the line.

Finally, thought Taylor. She turned and looked at Coach Tammy. "We're ready!"

"Here we go," said Coach Tammy. She started walking down the wide hallway that circled the arena.

Sarah and Jess started a cheer.

"Big D Elite, can't be beat!"

Taylor and Abby joined in.

"Big D Elite, can't be beat!"

The girls on both squads cheered as they walked around the wide hallway of the arena. Cheerleaders from other gyms looked at them as they walked by.

Yes, we are the ones to beat, thought Taylor.

When they reached the far side of the gym, Coach Tammy turned and led them into the narrow hallway. Now they were entering the arena.

"Big D Elite, can't be beat!"

Sarah and Jess cheered as they walked into the warm-up area.

I hope that's true, thought Taylor. *I hope Sophia isn't right.*

More Minis

Taylor looked up as they entered the arena. A long black curtain hung from the ceiling. It separated the floor of the arena into two parts. One side was for performing, and the other side was for practicing.

The parents were in the stands on the performing side. All of the parents from the Big D Elite gym sat together. They wore white T-shirts that said *Big D Elite* in red letters. Next to that was the gym's logo, a blue cowgirl boot.

Taylor's mom had made a sign with Taylor's name on it. The letters were made of red glitter. She'd put a blue cowgirl boot on the sign, too. It had silver glitter all around it. Taylor's mom always held up the sign when Taylor came out to cheer. It was so exciting!

Coach Tammy led the girls to the practice side of the arena. She took a sheet of paper out of her jeans pocket and unfolded it. "Let's see," said Coach Tammy. "Glow warms up next. Glitter warms up in 30 minutes."

The tinies always performed first. It was like that at every competition: The program always went from youngest to oldest. The youngest were first, and the oldest were last.

Coach Tammy waved at Miss Nancy. She was sitting up in the stands on the practice side. Miss Nancy ran the office at the Big D Elite gym. She owned the gym with her son Beau and her daughter Jen. Coach Beau and Coach Jen worked with the older girls.

Miss Nancy stood up and walked down to the floor. "You go on now, Tammy," said Miss Nancy. "I'll watch the minis while you warm up the tinies."

Taylor smiled. Miss Nancy was so nice.

Coach Tammy took the tinies to warm up. The Glitter team sat down on the floor by Miss Nancy. Taylor looked over as the other mini teams came in.

"Look at all the minis," said Taylor.

"There were only two other mini teams last year," said Abby.

"I wonder how many there are this year," said Taylor. She started counting. "One, two, three, four."

"And we're five," said Abby.

"Five!" said Taylor. "That's a lot!"

Taylor turned and looked at Sophia. Sophia was frowning as she looked at the other minis. *Why was she so upset?*

"Wait a minute!" said Taylor. "If there are five teams, then someone will be in fifth place."

"Fourth place, too," said Abby.

"But we came in second last year," said Taylor.

"Someone has to be last," said Abby.

"But not us," said Taylor.

"No, not us," said Abby. "Remember our cheer? Big D Elite ..."

"Can't be beat!" said Taylor. But someone had to be last. And now there were four other teams.

Taylor looked at Sophia again. *Is that why she's so upset? Does she think that I will make us last? My back walkover isn't that slow.*

CHAPTER 4
Practice

Taylor looked at the two long mats at the far end of the arena floor. No one was using them. *I can practice my back walkover while I wait. Miss Nancy won't mind.*

Taylor walked over and started her back walkover. First she did a bridge. She lifted her arms up and over her head. Then she arched back and put them on the floor behind her.

The bridge kickover was next. She lifted her right leg up. Then she kicked her left leg up. Taylor did the splits in the air. Then she moved her legs over one at a time and stood up. She lifted her arms into the air again. *Ta-da!*

Sophia walked over to the mat. "You're still too slow," said Sophia.

"No, I'm not," said Taylor.

"Yes, you are," said Sophia. "Do it again, and I'll count."

"No," said Taylor. "You do it, and I'll count."

"Easy peasy," said Sophia. She put up her arms. Then she did a bridge.

Taylor counted. "One, two, three, four."

Sophia kicked up her legs. Then she did the splits and stood up.

"Five, six, seven, eight," counted Taylor.

"See," said Sophia. "I did it in eight. Now you try."

"Okay," said Taylor. She put up her arms. She did a bridge.

"One, two, three, four, five," counted Sophia.

Taylor lifted up her legs and did the splits.

"Six, seven, eight, one," counted Sophia.

Taylor lifted her legs over her head and touched the floor.

"Two, three, four," counted Sophia.

Taylor stood up and put her arms in the air.

"Five," said Sophia. She brushed her hands like she was wiping away dirt. "I told you it was too slow."

"I'm not slow," said Taylor.

"Eight and five are thirteen," said Sophia.

"Thirteen!" said Taylor. "You're counting too fast."

"No, I'm not," said Sophia. She put her hands on her hips.

Abby came over and stood next to Taylor. "Let me count."

"That's better," said Taylor.

"You two can do it at the same time," said Abby.

"That's how we always do it," said Sophia. She pointed at the mat. "Come stand in your place, Taylor."

"I know what to do," said Taylor. She walked over and stood next to Sophia.

"Here we go," said Abby. She started counting. "Five, six, seven, eight."

After Abby said eight, Sophia and Taylor started their bridge.

"One, two, three, four," said Abby.

Sophia lifted her legs and did the splits.

"Five, six," said Abby.

Taylor lifted up her legs. Sophia kicked her legs over.

"Seven, eight," said Abby.

Sophia stood up. Taylor was still kicking her legs over.

"One, two, three," said Abby.

Taylor stood up.

"I told you you were too slow," said Sophia.

"But I'm not," said Taylor.

"Eight and three are eleven," said Sophia.

"It was thirteen last time," said Taylor.

"It's still too slow," said Sophia. "Tick tock, Taylor. You have to move faster if we're going to win!"

CHAPTER 5
Perfect!

"Oh, she makes me so mad," said Taylor.

"Don't worry about her," said Abby. "Coach Tammy is the boss, not Sophia."

"I know," said Taylor. "Look, here she comes."

Coach Tammy led the tinies back to the practice area. They had just finished performing.

"How did it go?" asked Miss Nancy.

"They were wonderful, as usual," said Coach Tammy.

Miss Nancy smiled. She walked up to each girl and gave her a hug. "Now come with me," said Miss Nancy. "Let's go find your parents. Then you can watch the other girls cheer."

Taylor watched as Miss Nancy, Sarah, and Jess walked the tinies down the narrow hallway. Each of them was holding a shiny trophy.

Clap, clap, clap!

Coach Tammy clapped her hands. "We practice next, Glitter, so line up."

Taylor ran over and stood by Abby. Sophia stood behind Taylor.

"Move faster this time," said Sophia.

Taylor turned and looked at Sophia. "Okay, okay. I get it."

"Here we go," said Coach Tammy. She started walking to the large practice mat. The other team had just finished. They were going over to the stage line.

The Glitter girls walked in line, two by two. They walked onto the mat in their double line, then each girl walked over and took her place. Taylor put her hands on her hips. Then she put her head down and waited for the music.

"Five, six, seven, eight," said Coach Tammy. The music started.

After a few notes played, a deep voice said, "Presenting ... Big D Elite Glitter!"

That was their cue. Taylor lifted her head and smiled. The Glitter girls did a back limber, row by row. Brianna and Emma did it first. Then Liv and Kayla did it. Taylor,

Abby, Maddie, and Sophia did it last.

After they finished, the girls ran to their places for the two stunts. Taylor was a base. She helped lift Brianna into the air for the stunts.

Cartwheels and the four jumps were next. Then more cartwheels and some forward rolls. The last roll brought Taylor to the center of the mat. It was time for the back walkover. Taylor stood next to Sophia.

Taylor counted softly, "Five, six, seven, eight."

Taylor lifted up her arms. Then she quickly did her bridge.

Hurry! Hurry!

Taylor lifted her legs and did the splits in the air.

Faster! Faster!

Taylor flipped her legs over and stood up ... just as Sophia came up.

Perfect!

CHAPTER 6
No More Crying

Clap, clap, clap!

Coach Tammy clapped her hands. Then she turned off the music.

Taylor turned to Sophia. "I did it."

"About time," said Sophia.

That's it? thought Taylor. *Nothing else? How about, you did a great job, Taylor. Or, that looks wonderful, Taylor.*

Wait, why did we stop? Taylor looked over at Coach Tammy. She was standing next to Brianna.

Oh! Brianna was crying again.

Taylor walked over to Abby. "Sophia's yelling upset Brianna," said Taylor. "I tried to stop it."

"You did stop it," said Abby.

"But she's still upset," said Taylor.

"Coach Tammy will calm her down," said Abby.

Taylor looked at Coach Tammy. She was hugging Brianna.

"That always works," said Abby.

"Coach Tammy is like a mom," said Taylor. She smiled.

Coach Tammy stood up. "Okay, Glitter," she said. "Let's do it again, from the top." She pointed at the edge of the mat.

The girls lined up at the edge of the mat again. Then they walked onto the mat and got into position.

Coach Tammy turned on the music. The girls did their back limbers, row by row.

Now for the stunts. Taylor ran over and stood behind Brianna. She held on to Brianna as they lifted her up for the stunt. *No crying! That's good.*

Taylor, Liv, and Maddie held Brianna up as they walked to the middle of the mat. Brianna reached out and grabbed Emma's hand.

Then the girls helped both flyers come down to the mat. It was cartwheel time! Taylor did two cartwheels across the mat. Then she ran to her spot for the four jumps.

Here we go! Taylor and the girls put their arms out to the side and touched their toes as they jumped into the air. Then they turned right and jumped facing the other side. One more turn and a jump facing the back. The last turn had them all facing the side. Once again they all jumped into the air at the same time.

Taylor did cartwheels until she reached the edge of the mat. Then she turned around and did three forward rolls. The back walkover was next.

I can do this, thought Taylor. She stood next to Sophia.

Arms up.

Back into the bridge.

Kick up.

Do the splits.

Legs over.

Stand up.

Arms up.

Taylor looked over at Sophia to see how far along she was. But Sophia wasn't there. *Wait a minute! Where is Sophia?*

Wait for Me

Taylor looked at the far side of the mat. Sophia was already doing the next move!

Taylor ran to the opposite side of the mat. She did another cartwheel, and then it was time for more stunts.

Taylor did a thigh stand and held up Liv. Liv lifted her other leg into the air. Then Liv came down.

Taylor and Liv ran over and helped Maddie lift Brianna. Then they walked

Brianna across the mat. Brianna reached
out and touched Emma's hand again.

That looked good, thought Taylor.

Brianna let go of Emma's hand. Taylor

and the other girls helped Brianna up as she did two more flyer moves.

And down you go. Taylor helped the girls lower Brianna down to the mat. Then all four girls ran to a new spot on the mat.

It's time for our cheer. Here we go, nice and loud!

"Big D Elite, can't be beat!

We're the ones you want to meet!"

After the cheer, Tyler walked over to the right side of the mat. *Up you go!* She helped Liv and Maddie lift Brianna up again. Brianna raised both of her arms into the air. *Nice!*

The girls brought Brianna back down. Then they did the dance moves.

One, two, three, four, arms out.

Five, six, seven, eight, arms up.

Hold that pose!

And then it was over. The music stopped.

Coach Tammy clapped her hands. "Great job, Glitter! Now it's time to line up and go on stage. The next squad is ready to use the mat."

Taylor looked at the minis waiting to use the mat. *I've never seen them before. I wonder how good they are.*

Sophia came up to Taylor. "What happened to you?" asked Sophia. She pointed her finger at Taylor. "Your back walkover was *way* too slow. I was already on the other side of the mat when you came up."

"I know," said Taylor. "I'm ..."

"You better get it right this time!" said Sophia. "We go on in a few minutes." She stormed off the mat.

Abby came over and hugged Taylor.

"Don't worry about Sophia," said Abby.

"But she's right," said Taylor. "I have to get it right next time."

"Do your best and forget the rest," said Abby. "That's what Coach Tammy says."

"But what if my best isn't good enough?" said Taylor. "I don't want to make us lose!"

Behind the Curtain

Taylor looked at the curtain. The squad ahead of them was on the mat right now. They were doing their routine as the music played. *I wish I could see them perform.*

The music stopped. Then the applause started. Taylor heard whistling and cheering from the audience on the other side.

We're next! Taylor looked at the Glitter girls lined up behind the curtain. Emma and Brianna were in front. Kayla and Liv stood behind them. *Then there's me and Abby.* She turned and looked at Sophia and Maddie at end of the line.

Sophia hissed, "You better get this right."

"I heard you the first time," said Taylor.

Sophia scowled. Taylor turned and looked at the curtain. Abby whispered in Taylor's ear, "I know you can do it."

Taylor nodded.

I wish Coach Tammy was here, thought Taylor. But she wasn't. Coach Tammy had gone out to give their music to the sound crew. And she wasn't coming back. Coaches stood next to the judges during the performance.

Oh, I hope I can do this! Taylor squeezed Abby's hand. Abby looked up and smiled.

"Are you ready?" asked the man with a clipboard.

I can do this, thought Taylor. *I can!*

The announcer said, "And now, it's Big D Elite Glitter!"

"You're on," said the man with a clipboard.

Brianna looked up at the man, but she didn't move.

"It's time to go, Brianna," said Emma. She pulled on Brianna's hand, but Brianna still didn't move.

"Go, Brianna!" hissed Sophia, from the back of the line.

Brianna turned. Her eyes opened wide.

"Why do you have to be so mean?" said Taylor. "We don't want her to start crying now."

"You think you're so good," said Sophia. "You get her to move." She pointed at Brianna.

"You don't have to be mean to get things done," said Taylor. She walked up to Brianna and gave her a hug.

"Coach Tammy is out there," said Taylor. "She's waiting to see you fly."

"She is?" said Brianna.

"We all want to see you fly," said Taylor. "I'll hold you up so you can fly. Liv and Maddie will, too."

"I like to fly," said Brianna.

"It's fun," said Taylor.

Brianna nodded her head.

"Go ahead," said Taylor. "Just like we do at practice. Walk out to the mat and smile."

"You can do it," said Abby.

"Okay," said Brianna. She nodded her head. Then she picked up Emma's hand. The two flyers started walking. Kayla and Liv followed.

Taylor waited for Abby. Then the two of them walked out toward the mat.

Sophia and Maddie came up behind them. "Don't be a slowpoke," said Sophia.

Doesn't anything make her happy? thought Taylor. She looked up as they walked under a bridge of orange and black balloons. They had decorated the stage for Halloween. Even the trophy table was decorated in orange and black. *And look at*

all those trophies! Oh, I hope we win one. I'm going to try. I can do this. I can!

When Emma and Brianna reached the middle of the mat, they turned and walked in a line down the center. All of the Glitter girls followed them.

Taylor looked up at the people sitting in the stands. *Where is Mom? Where are the Big D parents sitting?* Taylor looked around the arena. Then she heard the chanting, "Big D Elite, can't be beat!"

There they are! I see the white shirts. Oh! And there's my name! Taylor saw the sign with her name written in red glittery letters. Her mom waved the sign back and forth as she chanted with the other Big D parents. "Big D Elite, can't be beat!"

Taylor's smile got even bigger.

She walked over to her spot on the mat. She put her hands on her hips. Then she put her head down. *This is it!*

CHAPTER 9

Smile for the Judges

The music came on. After a few notes, a deep voice said, "Presenting ... Big D Elite Glitter!"

That was their cue! Taylor lifted her head and smiled for the judges.

The Glitter girls did their back limbers, row by row. Brianna and Emma were in the front row, so they went over first. Then Kayla and Liv went over next. Taylor was in the back row with Abby, Sophia, and

Maddie. They did their back limbers last.

Everyone ran to a new spot to start the first stunt. Taylor held on to Brianna as they lifted her up. Then all three bases walked to the middle of the mat. Taylor, Liv, and Maddie held Brianna up as she reached out for Emma's hand.

Smile for the judges, please, Brianna!

Taylor held on to Brianna as they lowered her back to the mat. Then they all began doing cartwheels. It looked like a flower growing, as the girls did their cartwheels out from the center of the mat.

Now the jumps! Taylor ran to her spot and faced forward. The squad jumped in the air facing the judges. Then they turned to the side and jumped again. Another turn and they jumped facing the trophies in the back. *I want one of those!* One last turn and they jumped facing the other side.

And over I go! Taylor did cartwheels to the edge of the mat. Then she turned and did three forward rolls back to the middle.

There's Sophia! It's time for the back walkover. I have to get this right!

Taylor stood next to Sophia.

Five, six, seven, eight, go!

Taylor reached her arms up.

She did the bridge.

Then she kicked up her legs.

Splits in the air.

Now over and up.

Taylor stood up *just* as Sophia did!

Taylor lifted her hands in the air. *I did it!*

Then she ran to the other side of the mat and kept going. She did a thigh stand and held on to Liv. Liv lifted her other leg into the air and did a heel stretch. *Great job!*

Taylor helped Liv come down. Then they ran over and helped Maddie with a new stunt. The girls lifted Brianna and carried her across the mat. Brianna reached out and touched Emma's hand again. *All right!*

Brianna let go of Emma's hand. Taylor and the other bases helped the flyers do two more moves. Each time she went up in the air, Brianna smiled for the judges.

The judges will like that! It's so much better when Brianna is happy.

Taylor helped Brianna back down to the mat. Then all four girls ran to their places for the cheer. When they started cheering, the parents and the other girls from the Big D Elite Gym joined in.

"Big D Elite, can't be beat. We're the ones

you want to meet!"

Wow! It sounded like everyone was cheering for Big D!

Taylor ran to right side of the mat for the last stunt. They lifted Brianna in the air one more time. *Go, flyer, go!*

And now for the dance.

One, two, three, four, arms out.

Five, six, seven, eight, arms up.

The music stopped. Taylor held the final pose. It was over.

CHAPTER 10
Applause!

The crowd erupted in applause. Taylor looked up at her mom. She was cheering and waving the sign with Taylor's name on it.

Yes, we did it!

A few seconds later, two grown-up cheerleaders came onto the blue mat. They pointed at the curtain on the other side. "The exit is that way."

Taylor turned and looked for Coach Tammy. She was walking in front of the judges. She had their music in her hand.

Now we can go. Taylor reached out and took Abby's hand. With her other hand, she took Brianna's hand, too. Abby took her sister Emma's hand. Together the four girls walked off the mat.

Coach Tammy joined the girls as they walked through the curtain. "Glitter, you were wonderful!"

Yay! Coach Tammy liked it.

Brianna let go of Taylor's hand and ran up to Coach Tammy for a hug. Coach Tammy hugged Brianna. Then she hugged Emma and Abby.

Taylor went over for a hug.

"You did a great job," said Coach Tammy.

"Thanks," said Taylor. She was so happy. Everyone was happy, everyone except Sophia. Sophia stood there with a frown on her face.

"We'll see what the judges say."

"Glitter, let's go sit with the other Big D girls," said Coach Tammy. And so they did. They went up and sat in the stands with the other squads from the Big D Elite Gym. They cheered for the youth squad, the juniors, and the seniors.

After all of the teams had performed it was time for the awards ceremony. The announcer asked all the cheerleaders to come down to the blue mat. All of the Big D Elite cheerleaders sat together.

"Ladies and gentlemen," said the announcer. "We want to welcome all of the new gyms that joined us this year."

Taylor looked around at the other girls on the mat. There were so many squads this year! *I hope we still have a chance!*

"This has been a great day of competition," said the announcer. You kept our judges quite busy." He walked over and picked up a plaque. "Let's begin with our minis." Taylor grabbed Abby's hand. Abby squeezed back.

"In fifth place," said the announcer, "the Spring Cheer Minis."

The Spring Cheer Minis cheered.

"It's not us," said Taylor. "We're not last." She looked over at Sophia. She wasn't frowning, but she wasn't smiling either.

The announcer picked up another plaque. "And in fourth place ..."

Taylor squeezed Abby's hand. "I hope he doesn't call us."

"Cheer Spirit Blue Stars," said the announcer.

The Cheer Spirit Blue Stars cheered.

"So far, so good," said Taylor.

"In third place," said the announcer.

Taylor held her breath.

"The Cheer Power Mini Cougars," said the announcer.

The Cheer Power Mini Cougars cheered.

"Only first and second are left," said Abby.

"That means we're first or second," said Taylor. "Cross your fingers!"

"On both hands," said Abby.

The two friends sat with their fingers crossed as the announcer picked up the next plaque.

"Second place goes to," said the announcer, and then he paused.

Who? Taylor squeezed her fingers tighter.

"All-Star Cheer Extreme Minis," said the announcer.

Taylor grabbed Abby's arm. "We did it!"

The announcer walked over and picked up the first place trophy. "And in first place," said the announcer, "Big D Elite Glitter!"

"YAY!" shouted Taylor. She jumped up, and the announcer put the first place trophy in her hands. All of the Glitter girls were jumping and clapping and cheering.

Taylor hugged Abby. They jumped up and down with the trophy.

"Do your best," said Abby.

"And forget the rest," said Taylor.

"I knew you could do it," said Abby.

"We all did it together," said Taylor. She looked at the Glitter girls around her. Everyone was so happy. Even Sophia was smiling at last.

About the Author

Books have always been part of Anastasia Suen's life. Her mother started reading to her when she was a baby and took her to the library every week. She wrote her first picture book when she was eleven and has been writing ever since. She used to be an elementary school teacher, and now she visits classrooms to talk about being an author. She has published over 125 books, writes an Internet blog about children's books, and teaches writing to college students. She's never been a cheerleader, but she can yell really loud!

Read them all!

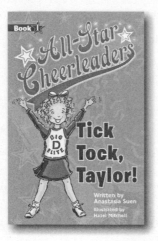